TWISTERS

Sally Sails the Seas

Stella Gurney
and Belinda Worsley

Evans

Sally sails the seas...

...past islands,
"Land!"

Through storms,
"Hold tight!"

Around whales, "Wow!"

She discovers maps, "Hmm"...

13

...and treasure, "Gold!"

15

She fights pirates, "Pow!"...

She sees monsters,
"Help!"...

...and mermaids,
"Nice hair!"...

...shipwrecks,
"Shame!"...

...and rubber ducks,
"Quack!"

Rubber ducks?

"Out you get, Sailor Sal!"

30

Why not try reading another Twisters book?

Not-so-silly Sausage by Stella Gurney and Liz Million
ISBN 0 237 52875 4
Nick's Birthday by Jane Oliver and Silvia Raga
ISBN 0 237 52896 7
Out Went Sam by Nick Turpin and Barbara Nascimbeni
ISBN 0 237 52894 0
Yummy Scrummy by Paul Harrison and Belinda Worsley
ISBN 0 237 52876 2
Squelch! by Kay Woodward and Stefania Colnaghi
ISBN 0 237 52895 9
Sally Sails the Seas by Stella Gurney and Belinda Worsley
ISBN 0 237 52893 2

If you liked Twisters try a ZigZag!

Dinosaur Planet by David Orme and Fabiano Fiorin
ISBN 0 237 52793 6
Tall Tilly by Jillian Powell and Tim Archbold
ISBN 0 237 52794 4
Batty Betty's Spells by Hilary Robinson and Belinda Worsley
ISBN 0 237 52795 2
The Thirsty Moose by David Orme and Mike Gordon
ISBN 0 237 52792 8
The Clumsy Cow by Julia Moffatt and Lisa Williams
ISBN 0 237 52790 1
Open Wide! by Julia Moffatt and Anni Axworthy
ISBN 0 237 52791 X
Too Small by Kay Woodward and Deborah van de Leijgraaf
ISBN 0 237 52777 4
I Wish I Was An Alien by Vivian French and Lisa Williams
ISBN 0 237 52776 6
The Disappearing Cheese by Paul Harrison and Ruth Rivers
ISBN 0 237 52775 8
Terry the Flying Turtle by Anna Wilson and Mike Gordon
ISBN 0 237 52774 X
Pet To School Day by Hilary Robinson and Tim Archbold
ISBN 0 237 52773 1
The Cat in the Coat by Vivian French and Alison Bartlett
ISBN 0 237 52772 3